The Easter Bunny

pictures *by* AGNÈS MATHIEU
story *by* WINFRIED WOLF

Dial Books for Young Readers · New York

Many people don't believe
in the Easter Bunny.
After all,
rabbits don't lay eggs, they tell me.

And how could a rabbit unlock
the bolt on his cage
and get out all by himself?
And where would he find a basket
to carry all his Easter eggs and gifts?

And everyone knows
that rabbits are afraid of people.
Why, as soon as they see you in the fields,
they speed away.
So you still think there's an Easter bunny?

Me too.
I think he's about the same height as you
with long, pointed ears.
He wears checkered pants as bright
as the eggs in his basket.
And he's very brave—in fact,
he travels alone all through the countryside.

I heard that once a fox saw him
running across the fields.
The fox hadn't eaten in days,
and a rabbit would have made him
very happy indeed.

But just in time the fox
saw it was the Easter Bunny.
"Sorry to have troubled you," he said.

There's another story
about a watchdog who was ready
to attack the strange rabbit
who wandered onto his farm.
But once he saw it was the Easter Bunny,
the dog just wagged his tail.

So, despite a few close calls,
the Easter Bunny still manages
to arrive safely at your front door.
But how does he get in?
He doesn't have a key!

It's simple.
His ears have special tips
that open any lock.

Once he's inside,
the Easter Bunny busies himself
doing what he likes best of all—
hiding eggs and presents
just for you.

If you're up early,
be sure to look out the window.
You just may see him scurrying
across the yard.
That is, *if* you believe in him.

First published in the United States 1986 by
Dial Books for Young Readers
A Division of Penguin Books USA Inc.
375 Hudson Street
New York, New York 10014

Published in West Germany by
Otto Maier Verlag Ravensburg as *Der Osterhase*
Copyright © 1984 by Otto Maier Verlag Ravensburg
This translation copyright © 1986 by
Dial Books for Young Readers
All rights reserved
Library of Congress Catalog Card Number: 85-10115
Printed in Hong Kong
First Pied Piper Printing 1991
E
1 3 5 7 9 10 8 6 4 2

A Pied Piper Book is a registered trademark of
Dial Books for Young Readers,
a division of Penguin Books USA Inc.,
® TM 1,163,686 and ® TM 1,054,312.

THE EASTER BUNNY
is published in a hardcover edition by
Dial Books for Young Readers.
ISBN 0-8037-0912-9